Biscuit's Christmas

A scratch-and-sniff book

story by Alyssa Satin Capucilli
pictures by Pat Schories

HarperFestival®
A Division of HarperCollinsPublishers

"Come along, Biscuit," called the little girl.
"Christmas is almost here.
It's time to choose our tree."
          Woof, woof!

"This tree is just the right size, Biscuit."
Woof, woof!
"Oh, Biscuit! You found a pinecone!"

"Mmm-mm! I smell hot chocolate!"
Woof, woof!

"Silly puppy!
How did you get those marshmallows?"

"We have everything we need
to trim the tree, Biscuit.
We have our friends, our family,
and lots of decorations."

Woof, woof!
"No, no, Biscuit!"
Bow wow!
"No tugging, Puddles!
The popcorn is for the tree!"

"It's time to put the star at the very top!"

Woof, woof!
"Wait, Biscuit!
Come back with that candy cane!"

"The stockings are hung.
Let's have some apple cider
and sing Christmas carols!"

Woof, woof!
"Biscuit, what are you doing?"

Woof, woof!
"Funny puppy, you are right!

I almost forgot to leave gingerbread and milk
for Santa Claus!"

"Oh, Biscuit, don't you just love the
sweet smells of Christmas?"